For The

Best

Person in

The

World

THIS BOOK WAS WRITTEN BY

....

....

....

YOU ARE GOOD AT

....

....

....

YOU ARE SUPER AWESOME BECAUSE

....

....

....

I WANT KNOW THAT YOU ARE

....

....

....

I LOVE HOW YOU

....

....

....

OUR FAVORITE THING
TO DO TOGETHER
IN SUMMER IS

....

....

....

YOU ALWAYS HELP ME TO

....

....

....

I LIKE WHEN YOU CALL ME

....

....

....

I LOVE WHEN
YOU COOK

....

....

....

YOU LAUGH A LOT WHEN I

. . . .

. . . .

. . . .

YOU ARE SMARTER THAN

....

....

....

YOU WORK HARD AT

....

....

....

I LOVE WHEN YOU

....

....

....

MY FAVORITE THING ABOUT YOU IS

....

....

....

IF I HAVE MILLION BUCKS
I WOULD BUY YOU

....

....

....

BEST THING ABOUT YOUR JOB IS

....

....

....

OUR FAVORITE THING TO DO TOGETHER IS

....

....

....

I WOULD BUY YOU
A MILLION

....

....

....

YOUR FAVORITE FOOD IS

....

....

....

YOU LOVE WHEN I

....

....

....

MOVIE/TV SHOW THAT WE BOTH LOVE IS

....

....

....

OUR FAVORITE THING
TO DO TOGETHER
IN WINTER IS

....

....

....

YOU ARE STRONGER THAN

....

....

....

YOU LOVE ME BECAUSE

....

....

....

I HAVE NEVER SEEN YOU

....

....

....

YOU ARE SPECIAL TO ME BECAUSE

. . . .

. . . .

. . . .

YOU MAKE EVERYONE

....

....

....

YOU WILL ALWAYS BE MY

....

....

....

YOU TAUGHT ME
HOW TO

....

....

....

I LOVE WHEN YOU TELL STORIES ABOUT

....

....

....

YOU INSPIRE ME TO DO

....

....

....

I ENJOYED A LOT WHEN WE WENT TO

....

....

....

I LOVE WHEN
WE PRANK

....

....

....

I LOVE YOU A LOT BECAUSE YOU NEVER

....

....

....

FUNNIEST THING
YOU DO IS

....

....

....

OUR FAVORITE THING TO DO TOGETHER IN SPRING IS

....

....

....

I WAS AMAZED WHEN YOU FIXED MY

....

....

....

I FEEL SAFE WHEN YOU

....

....

....

YOU DON'T CARE ABOUT

....

....

....

I'M PROUD TO SAY YOU ARE

....

....

....

YOU LIKE TO

....

....

....

OUR FAVORITE THING TO DO TOGETHER IN AUTUMN IS

....

....

....

I LOVED WHEN YOU SURPRISED ME WITH

....

....

....

YOU ALWAYS SAY

....

....

....

I LOVE YOU MORE THAN

....

....

....

GAME I LIKE TO PLAY WITH YOU IS

....

....

....

YOU ARE KIND OF PERSON WHO ALWAYS

....

....

....

YOU ARE PROUD OF ME WHEN I

....

....

....

YOU ARE A PERFECT

....

....

....

I WANT YOU TO KNOW THAT I WILL

....

....

....

I LOVE IT WHEN YOU

....

....

....